CW01582543

KANE &

IAN EDGINTON
WRITER

CHRISTOPHER MITTEN
ARTIST

RAMON PEREZ
INKER

TONY AVIÑA
COLORIST

SAIDA TEMOFONTE
LETTERER

BEN TEMPLESMITH & MARTIN EMBORG
COVERS

BEN TEMPLESMITH
COLLECTION COVER

CURTIS KING JR.
PUBLICATION DESIGN

SURREY LIBRARIES

Askews & Holts	16-Sep-2011
GRB	£14.99

Ben Abernathy Editor - Original Series | **Kristy Quinn** Assistant Editor - Original Series
Ian Sattler Director Editorial, Special Projects and Archival Editions | **Robbin Brosterman** Design Director - Books

Ben Abernathy Group Editor | **Hank Kanalz** Senior VP - Digital | **Bob Harras** VP - Editor in Chief

Diane Nelson President | **Dan DiDio** and **Jim Lee** Co-Publishers | **Geoff Johns** Chief Creative Officer
John Rood Executive VP - Sales, Marketing and Business Development | **Amy Genkins** Senior VP - Business and Legal Affairs
Nairi Gardiner Senior VP - Finance | **Jeff Boison** VP - Publishing Operations | **Mark Chiarello** VP - Art Direction and Design
John Cunningham VP - Marketing | **Terri Cunningham** VP - Talent Relations and Services
Alison Gill Senior VP - Manufacturing and Operations | **David Hyde** VP - Publicity
Jay Kogan VP - Business and Legal Affairs, Publishing | **Jack Mahan** VP - Business Affairs, Talent
Nick Napolitano VP - Manufacturing Administration | **Ron Perazza** VP - Online
Sue Pohja VP - Book Sales | **Courtney Simmons** Senior VP - Publicity | **Bob Wayne** Senior VP - Sales

KANE & LYNCH | Published by DC Comics. Cover, text and compilation Copyright © 2010, 2011 DC Comics. All Rights Reserved.

Originally published in single magazine form in KANE & LYNCH 1-6. Copyright © 2010, 2011 DC Comics. All Rights Reserved. KANE & LYNCH, Square Enix Ltd. and logo are trademarks of Square Enix Holdings Co. Ltd. All characters, their distinctive likenesses and related elements featured in this publication are trademarks of DC Comics. DC Comics does not read or accept unsolicited submissions of ideas, stories or artwork.

DC COMICS 1700 Broadway, New York, NY 10019 A Warner Bros. Entertainment Company
Printed by Quad/Graphics, Dubuque, IA, USA. 5|13|11. First printing. ISBN: 978-1-4012-3158-3

SUSTAINABLE FORESTRY INITIATIVE
Certified Chain of Custody
Promoting Sustainable Forest Management
www.sfiprogram.org
Fiber used in this product line meets the sourcing requirements of the SFI program. www.sfiprogram.org SGS-SFICOC-0130

CARACAS, VENEZUELA.
KANE... KANE, MAN...
YOU OKAY...YOU GOOD?

YEAH... I'M GOOD.

FORTY-FIVE MINUTES EARLIER.
SKTASSH
FUCK YOU, YOU BASTARD!
LEAVE ME ALONE!
JENNY, I JUST WANT TO TALK.
YOU'VE GOT NOTHING TO SAY I WANT TO HEAR!
GIVE ME A CHANCE...
WHY?! WHY SHOULD I?! AFTER ALL YOU'VE DONE!
BECAUSE I'M YOUR FATHER...

NO...NO... NO! YOU DO NOT HAVE THE RIGHT TO PULL THAT SHIT!
TEN YEARS... TEN YEARS YOU WERE GONE AND WE WERE HAPPY! WE HAD A LIFE, MOM AND ME...A MILLION MILES AWAY FROM THIS...THIS MACHO BULLSHIT--BUT YOU STILL MANAGED TO SCREW IT UP!
"THEY CAME AND GOT US IN THE MIDDLE OF THE NIGHT...THOSE ASSHOLES YOU RIPPED OFF...TO THEM WE WERE LEVERAGE, BUT TO YOU...WE WERE A LIABILITY!"
THAT'S NOT TRUE...
SMAK
I DON'T CARE!
"THEY KILLED HER! I HAD HER BLOOD AND BRAINS ON ME!"

THOSE MEN...THEY'RE GONE NOW, THEY CAN'T HURT YOU...YOU'RE SAFE.
ONLY BECAUSE YOU AND THAT PSYCHO YOU'RE WITH KILLED THEM ALL!
HEY! IF LYNCH HADN'T STEPPED UP, YOU'D BE DEAD IN A DITCH NEXT TO YOUR MOTHER! YOU'RE BUSTING MY BALLS BECAUSE HE SAVED YOUR LIFE!
I...
THE 7 WEREN'T JUST SOME GANG, THEY WERE A CRIMINAL ELITE...TOP MERCENARIES...
YOU SHOULD KNOW. YOU WERE ONE OF THEM!
I KNOW. THEY WERE MY FUCKING FAMILY. I RESPECTED THEM, TRUSTED THEM, AND THEY TURNED ON ME! I KILLED EVERY ONE OF THEM TO KEEP YOU SAFE!
LOOK, ONCE THE DUST SETTLES WE CAN DO WHATEVER YOU WANT, GO WHEREVER...
NO...
THEN WHAT DO YOU WANT?
TO GET AS FAR AWAY FROM YOU AS I CAN.
NOK NOK NOK

GO IN THE OTHER ROOM.
I THOUGHT YOU SAID...
GO!
LIKE SHIT ARE WE SAFE!
HEY, YOU READY? FIVE STAR OR NOT, I'M GOIN' STIR CRAZY IN THIS PLACE.
LYNCH...
I FIGURE WE'RE DUE SOME R&R NOW THEY'RE ALL TAKING A DIRT NAP. AND IT SEEMS LIKE A GODDAMN CRYIN' SHAME TO LEAVE ALL THEIR MONEY JUST LYING AROUND.
NOT NOW.
NO?
IT'S NOT A GOOD TIME. I'M TRYING TO STRAIGHTEN THINGS OUT WITH JENNY.
YEAH, I COULD HEAR.

I'LL BE IN THE BAR. YOU CHANGE YOUR MIND, COME FIND ME.
DON'T COUNT ON IT.
AS IF.
PUSSY.

IT'S OKAY, YOU CAN COME OUT NOW.
JENNY? OH FOR... JENNY, COME ON!
SON OF A BITCH! JENNY! *JENNY, OPEN THE GODDAMN DOOR!*
BRAKK KRAKK
NO...
NO!

SHIT!
HNN.
WHAT THE FUCK?!
THE GIRL. WHERE IS SHE?
THAT CRAZY WHORE, SHE...
GHK!
WHUD
OH GOD! DON'T KILL ME... PLEASE!
SAME QUESTION.
SHE... SHE TOOK OFF. STRAIGHT OUT THE DOOR AND DOWN THE HALL.

BDAMM
OH, NO...
"...JENNY!"
‹DRIVE!›
SON OF A BITCH!
KEYS!
YOU... CAN'T DO THIS!

WATCH ME.
WRRRRNN
SKREEE
BODAAKKK
UHH...

YOU KNOW, I REALLY LOVED THAT CAR, BUT FOR TEN MILLION DOLLARS, I THINK I'LL GET OVER IT.
HHH...
EASY MONEY!
CHOOMM
CHEK CHAK
CARE TO FUCKIN' ENLIGHTEN ME AS TO WHAT THE FUCK'S GOING ON?
GHKKKL...

STAY DOWN, SHIT-STAIN!
CHOOMM
GET IN.
WHERE ARE WE GOING?
TO GET MY GIRL!
VVRRRRNn
C'MON, CUT HER LOOSE. SHE DOESN'T WANT TO BE AROUND YOU. GET USED TO IT.
SUDDENLY YOU'RE DR. PHIL?! I DIDN'T ASK YOUR FUCKIN' OPINION!

THAT SO? WELL, I FIGURE WE'VE GOT BIGGER PROBLEMS RIGHT NOW! CHECK THIS OUT.
WHERE'D YOU GET THAT?
SAME PLACE AS THE BURNER. LET'S JUST SAY I HAD A LITTLE TROUBLE WITH THE ROOM SERVICE.
SHIT! SHIT *MOTHERFUCKIN'* ***SHIT!***
WHAT?
DON'T YOU GET IT? IT'S THE 7! THERE MUST BE A GODDAMN SCORCHED-EARTH CONTRACT OUT ON US! IN THE EVENT THEY ALL GET TAKEN DOWN, A TERMINATION PROTOCOL KICKS IN!
OUR DATA AND A SHIT-LOAD OF MONEY GETS DUMPED ON THE CIRCUIT AND IT'S A FREE-FOR-ALL. ANYONE WITH A GUN AND A PULSE GETS TO PLAY!
IT'S OPEN SEASON ON US.
GUESS THAT'S WHY THIS JACK-OFF CAME LOADED FOR BEAR!

HE'S NOT THE ONLY ONE. WE'VE GOT COMPANY. PLACE LIKE THIS, WORD SPREADS FAST.
IT'S THE GLOBAL RECESSION. PEOPLE ARE JUST DOING WHAT THEY GOTTA DO TO GET BY.
CHRIST, HOW MANY PILLS YOU POP TODAY?
ENOUGH... TO SMOOTH THINGS OUT. IT'S BEEN A WEIRD DAY.
TERRIFIC. HOLD ON.
WHAT GIVES?
"I CAN'T BRING THIS SHIT-STORM DOWN ON JENNY. I'VE GOT TO TAKE CARE OF BUSINESS FIRST.
YOU IN?
LIKE I'VE GOT A FUCKING CHOICE?

HANG BACK. THIS AIN'T NO RACE.
BUT IT DON'T MATTER, THEY KNOW WE'RE HERE, KNOW WE'RE ONTO THEM?
EXACTLY...
THAT'S WHY I DON'T WANNA BE THE FIRST GOIN' IN THERE...
"...BUT I WANNA MAKE DAMN SURE WE'RE THE LAST ONES WALKIN' OUT."
THRRRRRRRRTTTTTT

SPEKKA
TAKK
SPEKKA
TAKK
TAKKA
TAKK
HKKK...GKK....
FUCK! FUCK! FUCK!
GET US OUTTA HERE!
CHOOM
CHAK-CHEK
CHOOM
CHAK-CHEK

CHOOM
NO! NO!
VHRRRRMMMM
SKKKR
NNNGG

OUT-FUCKING-STANDING!
WE'RE NOT DONE YET.
DON'T WAIT FOR ME.
BRRAPP
NHH!
BASTARDS!
CHOOM
BDAMM
BDAMM
BDAMM
JESUS CHRIST! THEY'RE IN FRONT AND BEHIND!

GIAAHH!
CHOOM
SPLAKK
CHOOM
COME ON, COME ON... GODDAMMIT!
BRRAPP
BRRAPP
TIME TO DIE, MOTHERFUCKER! YOU GONNA MAKE ME A RICH MAN!

YOU GOT HALF THAT RIGHT!
BRRRAATT
UHK!
CHOOM
I'M OUT! LITTLE HELP HERE!
WHY DON'T YOU--
BRRRAATT
--CARRY YOUR OWN FUCKIN' WEIGHT FOR ONCE?!
LOOK INTO MY EYE!
UHH...
WHOA...

KANE... KANE, MAN. YOU OKAY... YOU GOOD?
YEAH... I'M GOOD.
SO WHAT DO WE DO NOW? EVERY PRICK WITH A RAP SHEET'S GOING TO BE GUNNING FOR US. WE'RE LIKE WINNIN' THE FUCKIN' LOTTERY. HOW THE HELL DO WE GET OUT OF THIS CRAP?
THE ONLY WAY... THE HARD WAY...
...WE FOLLOW THE MONEY.

CUBA.
THRRRRTTT
BRAKKA BRAKKA
BLAM
BLAM
BLAM
BLAM

GODDAMMIT! CAN'T YOU DRIVE THIS FUCKIN' THING STRAIGHT? I CAN'T GET A CLEAN SHOT!
DON'T BLAME ME! WE'RE SITTING ON THE 7'S MILLIONS AND YOU PICKED UP THIS CLUNKER!
BLAM BLAM BLAM
HEY, A LITTLE RESPECT. THIS IS AN AMERICAN CLASSIC!
NO, IT'S A HEAP OF SHIT!
THRR
RRRRRTTT
BRAKKA BRAKKA
TING
TENG
TANG
KTANG
SKKTASHH

JESUS!
RELAX, THIS IS A 1953 CHEVY BEL AIR, NOT SOME PIECE OF JAP CRAP LIKE THEY'RE DRIVING. SHE WAS BUILT TO LAST... SHE'S BUILT LIKE A FUCKIN' TANK!
THAT SO? THEN GRAB YOUR BALLS AND BUCKLE UP!
LET'S SEE HOW MUCH PUNISHMENT THIS BIG-BONED BITCH CAN TAKE!
SKREEEEE
AHH!

SKKTASHH
KDDUNKK
GNHK... HKKK... KKK....
NG... GGHN...

TOLD YOU.
SMART ASS!
VVRRRRRNN
VVRRRRRNNNNN
NHH... UHNH....
BDNNK-KDUNKK
GOD BLESS AMERICA!
"NEXT STOP, MIAMI!"

LATER.
YOU TRUST THESE GUYS?
I DON'T TRUST ANYONE, BUT WE NEED THEM. YOU DON'T LIKE IT, TONTO, BE MY GUEST AND SWIM HOME.
I'M JUST ASKING IS ALL. THEY LOOK AT ME THE WRONG WAY THOUGH, I'M PUTTIN' THEM DOWN.
YEAH, WELL, GO EASY ON THAT STUFF. I NEED YOUR HEAD IN THE GAME.
DON'T SWEAT IT... I'M GOOD TO GO.
SO, DO WE HAVE ANYTHING RESEMBLING A PLAN? YOU SAID FOLLOW THE MONEY BUT ALL WE'VE DONE THE LAST FEW DAYS IS COVER OUR ASSES AND RUN LIKE BASTARDS. NOTHING'S CHANGED!
WHEN WE GET STATESIDE... I'LL WORK SOMETHING OUT.
NO...NO, WE DO IT NOW. WE'RE IN THE MIDDLE OF THE OCEAN, NO ONE'S COMING FOR US SO WE'VE GOT A BREATHING SPACE, TIME TO COME UP WITH SOMETHING!
WE'VE BEEN LUCKY SO FAR, BUT WE CAN'T KEEP ON RUNNING. THAT TEN MIL BOUNTY'S PUT A BIG FAT TARGET ON OUR BACKS.

THEY DON'T EVEN HAVE TO BE CLEVER. THEY'LL JUST WEAR US DOWN. WE GET SLOPPY AND IT'S OVER. IT'S NOT A MATTER OF "IF" BUT "WHEN."
YOU SEEM TO BE ON A ROLL, HAVE YOU GOT ANY BRIGHT IDEAS HOW WE GET OUT FROM UNDER THIS ROCK?
ACTUALLY I DO...
CALL HIM. THE FUCKER WHO PUT THIS MARK ON US. CALL HIM AND WORK A DEAL. YOU'RE THE LAST OF THE 7, THAT'S GOT TO COUNT FOR SOMETHING?
IT'S HER NOT HIM-- AND NO, IT WON'T.
HER?
DR. ILSA SILBERMANN, THE 7'S LAWYER...THEIR CONSIGLIERE...BUT SHE'S MUCH MORE THAN THAT. SHE'S... A FACILITATOR. SHE OVERSAW AND COORDINATED EVERY JOB, EVERY HIT.
SHE KNOWS WHERE THE MONEY'S STASHED AND THE BODIES ARE BURIED.
IT'D BE A WASTE OF TIME.
SO WHAT HAPPENS WHEN THEY GO AFTER YOUR KID...IF THEY HAVEN'T ALREADY? USE HER TO GET TO YOU?
MAKE THE CALL. IT'S A SATELLITE PHONE. IT BELONGED TO THAT JERK WHO FELL THROUGH THE WINDOW. THE REWARD LINE'S ON SPEED DIAL.
TAKE IT, MAKE THE DAMN CALL.

BERLIN.
‹COME ON NOW, DINNER'S ALMOST READY. I WANT EVERYONE AT THE TABLE, HANDS WASHED, NICE AND CLEAN.›*
BDEEP-BDEEP BDEEP-BDEEP
* TRANSLATED FROM GERMAN.
‹HELLO, YES.›
‹DOCTOR, IT'S MATTHIAS. I'M SORRY TO DISTURB YOU BUT--›
‹WHY ARE YOU CALLING ME? YOU KNOW I DO NOT DISCUSS BUSINESS AT HOME. I AM WITH MY GRANDCHILDREN.›
‹DOCTOR, I HAVE KANE ON THE OTHER LINE.›
‹I...WHO DID YOU SAY?›
‹KANE, HE WISHES TO TALK WITH YOU.›
‹VERY WELL, PUT HIM THROUGH.›
DOCTOR SILBERMANN.
KANE, I WAS WONDERING WHEN YOU WOULD CALL. I IMAGINE YOU WANT TO NEGOTIATE A WAY OF CANCELLING THE CONTRACT AND CALLING OFF THE DOGS?

YOU SOUND AS IF YOU'VE MADE YOUR MIND UP ALREADY.
PUT IT ON SPEAKER. THIS IS ABOUT ME TOO.
PERCEPTIVE AS EVER, BUT IT'S GONE TOO FAR. I NEED TO MAKE AN EXAMPLE OF YOU, TO SHOW THAT DEAD OR ALIVE, THE 7 CANNOT BE TRIFLED WITH, THAT THERE ARE CONSEQUENCES.
WHAT'RE YOU TALKING ABOUT?! I'M STILL A MEMBER OF THE 7! I'M THE LAST MAN STANDING!
EXCEPT YOU RENEGED. YOU TURNED YOUR BACK ON THAT POSITION SOME TIME AGO.
THEY TRIED TO KILL ME!
I KNOW. IT WAS MY RECOMMENDATION.
YOU... YOU'RE NOT JUST TAKING CARE OF BUSINESS, ARE YOU...? YOU'RE TAKING OVER!
YOU ALWAYS WERE MORE ASTUTE THAN THE OTHERS. THEY WEREN'T EXACTLY BIG THINKERS. I IMAGINE THAT'S WHY THEY TURNED AGAINST YOU.
WITH YOU GIVING THEM A NUDGE ALONG THE WAY!
IT'S A PITY. IN MY NEW REGIME, SUCH TALENT WOULD BE REWARDED, NOT TREATED WITH SUSPICION AND TREACHERY.
WHAT ABOUT ME, Y'CRAZY FUCKIN' BITCH?! WHAT I EVER DO TO YOU?
YOU, MR. LYNCH, I DESPISE ON PRINCIPLE. KILLING YOU WOULD BE DOING THE WORLD A SERVICE.

THE THE 7 WAS A FINE CONCEPT POORLY EXECUTED...IF YOU'LL FORGIVE THE PUN. IT WAS MUCH MORE THAN MERE MERCENARIES AND ASSASSINS. IT WAS AN INTELLIGENCE GATHERING NETWORK WITHOUT PEER. YET IT WAS NEVER EXPLOITED AS SUCH, BUT WASTED ON TESTOSTERONE-FUELED VENDETTAS.
WHAT IT REQUIRES IS A WOMAN'S TOUCH.
THE JAPANESE HAVE A SAYING, "BUSINESS IS WAR," AND I MEAN BUSINESS, KANE. THAT SAID, I DO HAVE A PROPOSITION FOR YOU...
KILL LYNCH. TURN YOURSELF OVER TO MY PEOPLE AND I'LL GIVE THE TEN MILLION DOLLAR CONTRACT MONEY TO YOUR DAUGHTER... TO JENNY.
FROM WHAT I UNDERSTAND, YOU HAVEN'T BEEN MUCH OF FATHER TO HER...GETTING HER MOTHER MURDERED? THIS PERHAPS WOULD GO SOME WAY TO MAKING AMENDS?
YOU LEAVE HER ALONE! DON'T YOU FUCKIN' TOUCH HER!
CHAK-CHEK
SON OF A BITCH!

THROW YOUR GUNS OVER THE SIDE! GENTLY... GENTLY!
NOW, TOSS ME THE PHONE.
ON YOUR KNEES, HANDS BEHIND YOUR HEADS. CROSS YOUR ANKLES.
HELLO...HELLO? THIS IS CAPTAIN SOLANO... TELL ME MORE ABOUT THIS TEN MILLION DOLLARS.
SPEAKERPHONE... CHRIST! YOU ASSHOLE!
YOU'RE THE ONE WHO HIRED THESE MOTHERFUCKERS!
BESIDES, YOU COULD'VE JUST TOLD ME "NO" RIGHT?!

YEAH...YEAH. I... I WASN'T THINKING STRAIGHT.
IT'S THAT KID OF YOURS! YOU'VE GOTTA GET THAT DADDY SHIT OUT OF YOUR HEAD RIGHT NOW!
YOU CAN'T HELP HER IF YOU'RE DEAD!
HEADS UP. GAME TIME.
WELL NOW, WHEN YOU FIRST CAME TO ME, OFFERED ME FIFTY THOUSAND DOLLARS TO TAKE YOU TO MIAMI, I FIGURED IT WAS MY LUCKY DAY! I DIDN'T REALIZE EXACTLY HOW LUCKY I WAS GONNA BE!
TEN MILLION DOLLARS! BROTHER, YOU PISS THAT LADY OFF BIG TIME.
IT'S A TALENT I HAVE.
SHE WANTS YOU ALIVE... FOR NOW.
BUT YOU... FOR YOU IT'S OVER!
NO! WAIT...WAIT! DID SHE TELL YOU TO KILL HIM?
SHE TOLD YOU TO...AND THE CONTRACT...

BUT DID SHE TELL YOU SPECIFICALLY TO KILL HIM?
I KNOW HER, SHE'S A METHODICAL BITCH. YOU DON'T WANT TO GET ON HER WRONG SIDE.
SHE WANTS HIM DEAD, FINE, BUT NOW OR LATER? IT WON'T HURT TO LEAVE HIM BREATHING A FEW HOURS MORE.
IT'S A SWEET DEAL, YOU DON'T WANT TO SCREW IT UP OVER SOMETHING STUPID.
HM, LET'S ASK HER.
SHIT, BUSY! I GUESS IT'LL KEEP.
SO WILL YOU--
KRAKK
--FOR NOW.
CLDD
<MATTHIAS, CONTACT COOGAN IN MIAMI. SOME LOW-LIFE'S BRINGING KANE IN-->

"‹I WANT HIM MET AND DEALT WITH ACCORDINGLY.›"
THIS LOOKS LIKE THE END OF THE LINE, MY FRIENDS.
ARE YOU FROM THE LADY DOCTOR?
NO, WE'RE COLLECTING FOR THE RED CROSS! YOU GOT THE MEAT?
A LITTLE BRUISED, BUT THEY'RE IN ONE PIECE. YOU HAVE MY MONEY?
SURE, HOLD ON. IT'S OKAY...

KABLAM
NO...
KABLAM
UTT!
THANKS, MY MAN. NICE WORK.
AMATEURS!
DR. SILBERMANN SAYS HI.

HI YOURSELF.
SPAKK
WHAT DID YOU DO?
IT WASN'T...
KRAKK
SPAKK
CHAKK
JESUS CHRIST!

I GUESS SOMEONE UP THERE LIKES US!
OR HATES THE 7 A WHOLE LOT MORE. EITHER WAY, I'M NOT HANGING AROUND TO FIND OUT.
UHNNH
WHERE THE FUCK ARE THEY?
THRRRTT
WHO ARE YOU SHOOTING AT?
BRAKKABREKK
I DON'T SEE A GODDAMN ONE!
SPAKKA
SPEKK
SPAKK

SCREW THIS! LET'S GO!
VVRRRRNN
KASHOOOMM

CHRIST ALL-FUCKING-MIGHTY! WHO ARE THOSE GUYS?
I THINK WE'RE ABOUT TO FIND OUT.
LOSE THE PIECES... NOW.
ANYTHING YOU SAY.
SHUT THE FUCK UP!

HIT THEM.
T-ZZAK
T-ZZAK
NNGG!
GKKK!
THEY'RE OUT. PACK THEM UP.
YOU'D BETTER BE WORTH IT.

HHH...
WHU...
YOU'VE GOTTA BE KIDDING!

SMOOTH.
KNOCK KNOCK
YEAH?

MR. LYNCH. IF YOU'LL FOLLOW ME, PLEASE.
SURE.
YOU GOING TO TELL ME WHAT'S GOING ON HERE?
I'M AFRAID NOT, SIR, NOT MY JOB. BUT I'VE NO DOUBT YOU'LL FIND OUT SOON ENOUGH.
THIS IS SOME PLACE.
INDEED.
SO, WHAT'S TO STOP ME JUST WALKING OUT OF HERE?
A STRONG SENSE OF SELF-PRESERVATION.

HELP YOURSELF TO TEA OR COFFEE. MR. HENDRYKS WILL BE ALONG SHORTLY.
WELL, I'VE WOKEN UP IN SOME SHIT-HOLES BEFORE NOW, BUT THIS I COULD GET USED TO. THIS IS SOME SERIOUSLY WEIRD FUCKED-UP SHIT.
IT'S ALSO PROBABLY WIRED. SOUND AND VISION, SO WATCH WHAT YOU SAY.
THAT'S TOO BAD, 'CAUSE I LEFT MY DICK TRACY DECODER RING IN MY OTHER PANTS AND I'M NOT IN THE MOOD FOR AWKWARD SILENCES!
SO, WHY AREN'T WE DEAD? FOR TEN MILLION DOLLARS, WE SHOULD BE DEADER THAN MEL GIBSON'S CAREER!
BECAUSE WE'RE WORTH MORE TO THIS...HENDRYKS ALIVE. WORTH SAVING OUR ASSES, DOPING US UP, FLYING US HALF-WAY AROUND THE WORLD...
...AND KITTING US OUT IN SUITS THAT COST MORE THAN MY LAST APARTMENT.
YOU'RE SHITTING ME!
NO, MR. LYNCH. HE'S NOT...

ALTHOUGH IT IS MR. KANE I AM INTERESTED IN. YOU, I AM KEEPING UNDER SUFFERANCE FOR NOW. HOWEVER, VEX ME AND I'LL HAVE LILA PUT YOU DOWN LIKE A DOG, IS THAT CLEAR?
AND RUIN A SUIT LIKE THIS? THAT'D BE A GODDAMN SHAME!
THEN, PLEASE, BE SEATED.
HAVE WE MET?
IT'S QUITE POSSIBLE. I POSSESS A BROAD RANGE OF BUSINESSES WHICH DO ON OCCASION STRADDLE ILLEGALITY. IT'S WHY I HAVE GONE TO THE TROUBLE OF BRINGING YOU HERE...
YOU SEE, I WANT ACCESS TO THE 7.
I HATE TO BREAK IT TO YOU, BUT YOU'RE SHIT OUT OF LUCK! THOSE BASTARDS ARE ALL TAKING A WORM BATH!
I WARNED YOU. THAT IS STRIKE ONE!

YOU AND DOCTOR SILBERMANN ARE ALL THAT REMAINS OF THAT ORGANIZATION-- AND SHE IS PROVING MOST INTRACTABLE TO DEAL WITH.
TELL ME ABOUT IT... BUT LIKE HE SAID, THE 7'S AS GOOD AS GONE.
NOT ALL. NOT YET. I AM A BUSINESS MAN, MR. KANE. MERGERS. ACQUISITIONS. HOSTILE TAKEOVERS. I EMPLOY WHATEVER RESOURCES ARE REQUIRED TO ATTAIN MY GOALS, LEGAL OR OTHERWISE.
WITH THE 7 DIMINISHED, THERE IS A POWER VACUUM. NOW IS THE TIME TO MOVE IN AND TAKE OVER, BEFORE CHAOS ENSUES AS SUNDRY GROUPS JOSTLE TO FILL THE VOID.
I WANT THE 7...AND I WANT YOU TO RUN IT FOR ME.
ME?!
IT'S THE OPPORTUNITY OF A LIFETIME. FEW MEN ARE OFFERED SUCH POWER.
IF DR. SILBERMANN HADN'T REFUSED TO NEGOTIATE WITH ME, YOU WOULD NO DOUBT BE LYING FACE DOWN IN THE GUTTER WITH A HOLE THE SIZE OF A FIST IN YOUR HEAD.
HER LOSS IS YOUR GAIN, PROVIDED YOU ARE WISE ENOUGH TO APPRECIATE IT AS SUCH.
WHAT HAVE I GOT TO DO?

UNFORTUNATELY IT'S NOT AS STRAIGHTFORWARD AS REMOVING THE GOOD DOCTOR. WE NEED TO KNOW WHAT SHE KNOWS, HOW TO ACCESS THE DATABASES SHE ESTABLISHED AND SO ON.
FOR THAT WE NEED LEVERAGE...WE NEED HER GRANDCHILDREN.
NO...NO, KIDS.
FOR A KILLER, YOU HAVE AN ALARMING STREAK OF MORALITY RUNNING THROUGH YOU.
PERMIT ME TO PROVIDE YOU WITH AN INCENTIVE. LILA, IF YOU PLEASE...
JENNY!
OH, FOR CHRIST'S SAKE! NOT THAT BITCH AGAIN!
THAT'S STRIKE TWO!

CHAK-CHEK
HEY, HEY WAIT A MIN--
HA! HA! HA! I'M JOKING. IT'S OKAY, YOU CAN HAVE THAT ONE!
WHERE IS SHE? WHERE DID YOU TAKE THESE?
ALL IN GOOD TIME. AS YOU CAN SEE, I CAN GET TO HER ANY TIME. I HATE TO RESORT TO OBVIOUS THREATS BUT IT IS A SIMPLE CHOICE...HER OR THEM.
ALL RIGHT... I'M IN.

GOOD. I KNEW WE COULD WORK THINGS OUT. NOW, AS TO PRACTICALITIES...
THEY CAN WAIT. I WANT OUT OF HERE FIRST. I WANT SOME AIR.
AND A DRINK!
SIR, THAT'S NOT A GOOD IDEA.
NO...NO, I DON'T THINK THEY'LL DO ANYTHING RASH. AND AS FAR AS THE CRIMINAL FRATERNITY IS CONCERNED, THEY'RE OUT OF THE PICTURE.
"I THINK WE CAN AFFORD TO RISK LETTING OUT THEIR LEASH A LITTLE."
BL D BEGGAR
WE CAN'T TRUST HIM.
WHAT'S THIS "WE" CRAP, COMPADRE? YOU'VE BEEN OFFERED A SEAT ON THE FUCKING BOARD, WHILE I'M STILL A FUCKING MOVING TARGET!

IT'S ALL BULLSHIT, HE'S PLAYING ME, I KNOW IT. IT'S HIS GAME, IT'S WHAT HE DOES... I KNOW WHO HE IS.
WHAT'RE YOU TALKING ABOUT?
HE'S HAD WORK--SURGERY--BUT I KNOW THAT FACE, HIS VOICE. HE CALLS HIMSELF HENDRYKS NOW...
"BUT FIFTEEN YEARS AGO HE WAS KONRAD LEMAS--THE BUTCHER OF BOSNIA.
"HE AND HIS MEN WERE MERCS HIRED BY THE SERBS FOR ADDITIONAL FIREPOWER, BUT LEMAS SAW A WAY TO TURN A PROFIT ON THEIR ETHNIC CLEANSING.
"THEY MADE OUT THEY WERE A UNITED NATIONS MEDICAL FIELD UNIT. EVACUATED WHOLE VILLAGES WITH PROMISES OF INOCULATING THEM AGAINST A SUPPOSED OUTBREAK OF TUBERCULOSIS.
"THEY EUTHANIZED THOUSANDS AND HARVESTED THEIR ORGANS FOR SALE.
"HE THEN PAID HIS MEN OFF WITH A HOLLOW-POINT HANDSHAKE."

HOW D'YOU KNOW ALL OF THAT?
I JUST DO, OKAY.
SO, WHAT DO WE DO NOW?
NOTHING. THERE ARE EYES ON US. WE HAVE TO PLAY ALONG FOR THE MOMENT.
YEAH, WELL I GOTTA GO PISS. THOUGH THE WAY THIS BEER TASTES, I MAY AS WELL JUST THROW IT DOWN THE JOHN AND CUT OUT THE MIDDLE MAN.
ALL RIGHT, GEEZER. I'LL SEE YOU LATER, YEAH? NO WORRIES, IT'S PAY DAY, I'M MINTED!

WHUDDTCH
GKKL
IT'S LYNCH.
TELL THAT BITCH
I WANT TO CUT
A DEAL...

BERLIN, THREE DAYS LATER.
"TELL HER I'VE GOT SOMETHING SHE'LL WANT TO HEAR."
<TROUBLE?>*
<NO, THIS IS ALWAYS A BAD JUNCTION. IT'S OKAY, I KNOW ANOTHER WAY AROUND.>
*TRANSLATED FROM GERMAN.

SKITTSHH
SKREEEE
GO! GO!
‹SHIT! BACK UP! BACK UP!›
UHK...
BAM BAM BAM

GHN...
BLAM BLAM
DOCTOR SILBERMANN, IT LOOKS LIKE LYNCH'S INTEL WAS CORRECT. THEY'RE MAKING THEIR MOVE EXACTLY WHERE YOU ANTICIPATED.
AND IS LYNCH THERE?
THERE'S NO MISTAKING HIM, AS AGREED.
TAKE THEM OUT, MATTHIAS. ALL OF THEM.
LYNCH, TOO? I THOUGHT YOU HAD AN ARRANGEMENT?
SO DOES HE. I IMAGINE THIS WILL COME AS QUITE A SURPRISE.

‹DON'T MOVE. BE COOL AND YOU WON'T GET HURT.›
‹OUT! OUT NOW, C'MON!›
‹DIDN'T YOU HEAR WHAT I SAI--SHIT!›
BRRRAATT
BRRRAPPA
IT'S A SET-UP!

BRRRAATT
BRRAPP
BREKK
GNHK... HKKK... KKK....
TEKK TAKKA TENGG TAKKA TENGG
GNHK... HKKK... KKK....
AGH!
SKRIKK
NG... GGHN...

‹YOU REALLY ARE TOO TRUSTING!›
‹IT'LL BE THE DEATH OF YOU.›
BLAM BLAM BLAM
FUCKIN' BITCH!
GET INSIDE! THIS THING'S ARMORED UP!
SPAKK
TAKK
TEKK

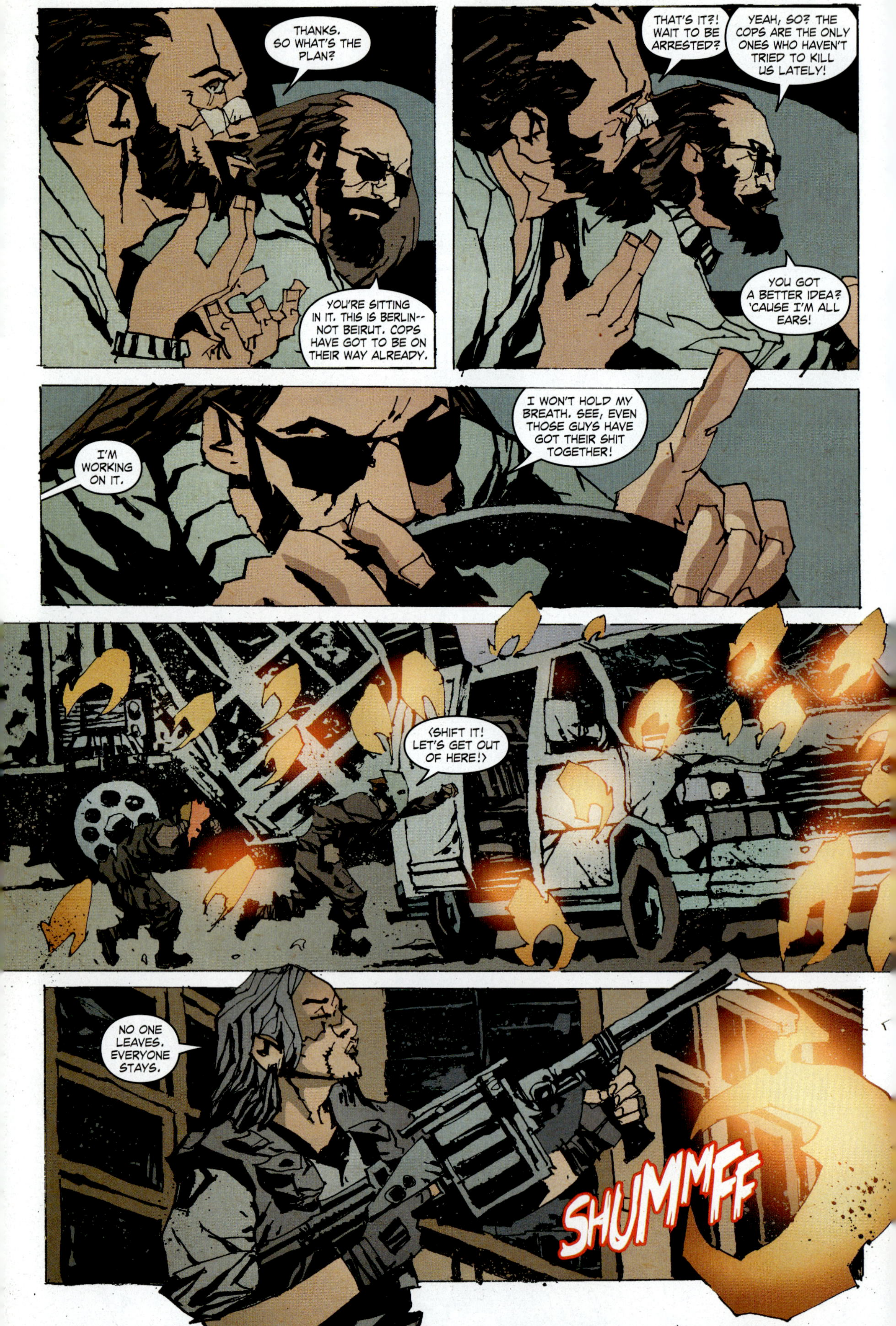
THANKS. SO WHAT'S THE PLAN?
YOU'RE SITTING IN IT. THIS IS BERLIN-- NOT BEIRUT. COPS HAVE GOT TO BE ON THEIR WAY ALREADY.
THAT'S IT?! WAIT TO BE ARRESTED?
YEAH, SO? THE COPS ARE THE ONLY ONES WHO HAVEN'T TRIED TO KILL US LATELY!
YOU GOT A BETTER IDEA? 'CAUSE I'M ALL EARS!
I'M WORKING ON IT.
I WON'T HOLD MY BREATH. SEE, EVEN THOSE GUYS HAVE GOT THEIR SHIT TOGETHER!
‹SHIFT IT! LET'S GET OUT OF HERE!›
NO ONE LEAVES. EVERYONE STAYS.
SHUMMFF

FA-SHOOMM
JESUS-FUCKIN-H!
WE'RE NEXT! DRIVE!
DRIVE, YOU ASSHOLE!
THUNN
FA-SHOOMM
VVRRRRNN

NNFF...
KEEP GOING!! FLOOR IT!
THRRUNNN
BA-KOOMM
KDUN KRUN KRUN KDUN KRUNK
SON-OF-A BITCH!
THUNN
HARD OVER!

CHOOM
VVRRRUMMM
‹SHIT!›
NICE TOUCH.
I THOUGHT SO.

WHAT THE FU--
DID YOU SELL US OUT?
WHAT?!
YOU USE THAT THING, WE'RE BOTH DEAD!
I'LL TAKE THAT CHANCE. SO, DID YOU SELL US OUT?
NO...FUCK NO. C'MON--I SAVED YOUR ASS BACK THERE!
OKAY. JUST CHECKING.
SHIT, THIS IS TURNING INTO ONE HELL OF A DAY.
IT'S GOING TO GET BETTER... I'VE GOT A PLAN TO GET THE 7 OFF OUR BACKS...
YOU'RE GOING TO CONTACT THEM AND OFFER TO TURN ME IN FOR THE BOUNTY.

AHUH-HUH AHHUH!
POK
POK
KRAUT FUCKERS!
BDAMM BDAMM BDAMM

GAH!
SPUKK
HAH! HAH! HAH! ADIOS, ASSHOLES!
NFF!
KDUNNK
HHH...
‹KICK THE SHIT OUT OF HIM›*
*TRANSLATED FROM THE GERMAN.
TANG
TENNG
TAKA
TAKK
SKTASHH
‹SHIT!›

GET OFF YOUR ASS AND IN THE CAR, YOU DUMB FUCK!
FLOOR IT!
TEKK KTANG TEKK
SPTANG
YOU GOT IT? YOU HAPPY NOW? YOU GONNA STOP WHINING?
OH, YEAH... BREAKFAST OF GODDAMN CHAMPIONS!
JESUS CHRIST.
KTNK

I NEED A VACATION.

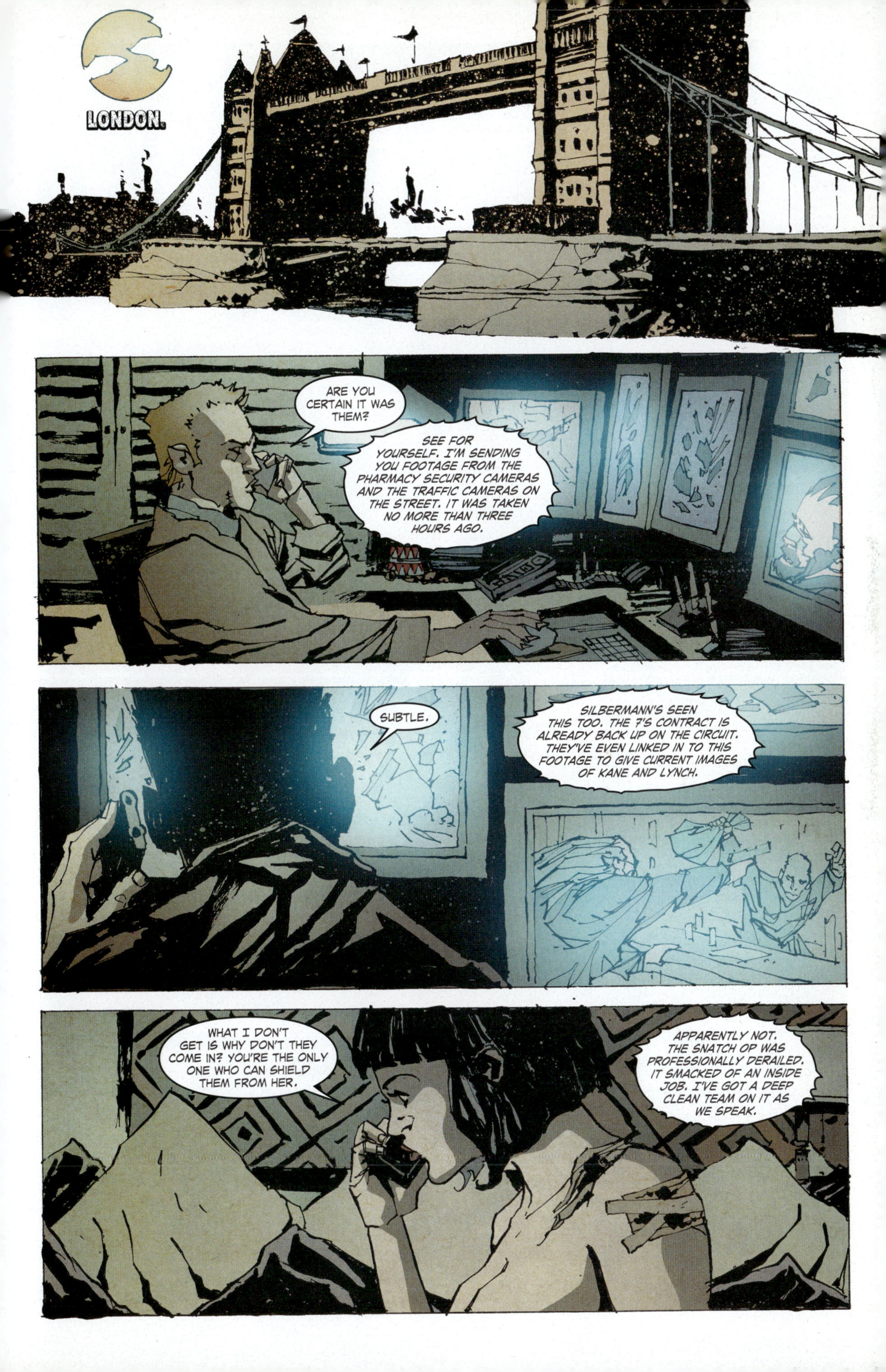
LONDON.
ARE YOU CERTAIN IT WAS THEM?
SEE FOR YOURSELF. I'M SENDING YOU FOOTAGE FROM THE PHARMACY SECURITY CAMERAS AND THE TRAFFIC CAMERAS ON THE STREET. IT WAS TAKEN NO MORE THAN THREE HOURS AGO.
SUBTLE.
SILBERMANN'S SEEN THIS TOO. THE 7'S CONTRACT IS ALREADY BACK UP ON THE CIRCUIT. THEY'VE EVEN LINKED IN TO THIS FOOTAGE TO GIVE CURRENT IMAGES OF KANE AND LYNCH.
WHAT I DON'T GET IS WHY DON'T THEY COME IN? YOU'RE THE ONLY ONE WHO CAN SHIELD THEM FROM HER.
APPARENTLY NOT. THE SNATCH OP WAS PROFESSIONALLY DERAILED. IT SMACKED OF AN INSIDE JOB. I'VE GOT A DEEP CLEAN TEAM ON IT AS WE SPEAK.

SIR, WITH RESPECT. THERE'S MORE GOING ON HERE THAN MEETS THE EYE. KANE KNOWS YOU CAN GET TO HIS DAUGHTER--YOU'VE GOT HIM BY THE BALLS.
EVEN IF THERE IS A TRAITOR OR MOLE OR GOD KNOWS WHAT, HE'D STILL RISK HIS NECK AND COME BACK IN TO SAFEGUARD HIS KID. HE'S THAT KIND OF MAN.
HE'S STAYING OUT IN THE COLD FOR A REASON. I THINK HE'S...
WHEN I WANT YOUR OPINION, MISS BATAILLE, I'LL GIVE IT TO YOU. IS THAT CLEAR?
YES, SIR. SO... WHAT ARE YOUR ORDERS?
I'VE DISPATCHED ANOTHER TEAM TO YOUR LOCATION. YOU ARE TO LIAISE WITH THEM, LOCATE KANE AND LYNCH, AND KILL THEM. REDUCE THEM TO NOTHING BUT A STAIN AND A MEMORY, IS THAT CLEAR?
YES, SIR.
IT WAS AN OUTSIDE SHOT THAT KANE COULD DELIVER ME THE 7. HE ALWAYS WAS AN OBSTINATE BASTARD. I'LL TAKE DOWN SILBERMANN IN MY OWN WAY AND MY OWN TIME.
CALL ME WHEN YOUR CREW ARE READY TO ROLL.
UNDERSTOOD.
CLICK
KANE...

BERLIN.
I AM DISAPPOINTED IN YOU, MATTHIAS, VERY DISAPPOINTED.
I APOLOGIZE, DOCTOR SILBERMANN. IT WILL NOT HAPPEN AGAIN.
AND WHAT MAKES YOU THINK I WILL GIVE YOU A SECOND CHANCE? THAT YOU WILL STILL BE ALIVE COME THE END OF THE DAY?
I DO NOT TOLERATE FAILURE LIGHTLY. IT REFLECTS BADLY ON MYSELF. IT REFLECTS BADLY ON THE 7. WE HAVE A STANDARD TO UPHOLD.
THEN PLEASE, ALLOW ME TO CORRECT MY ERROR. KANE AND LYNCH WILL NOT ESCAPE ME A SECOND TIME.
AND IT IS OUT OF RESPECT FOR YOUR LOYAL SERVICE THAT I WILL PERMIT YOU TO DO SO. NOW, WHAT DO WE KNOW?
SINCE WE REINSTATED THE BOUNTY ON THEM, FEEDBACK HAS BEEN MOST PROMISING. THE RAID ON THE PHARMACY EARLIER THIS MORNING PLACES THEM STILL WITHIN IN THE CITY. I HAVE PEOPLE ON THE GROUND FOLLOWING LEADS IN THE AREA ALREADY.
WATCH FOR LYNCH... HE'S THE ONE. HE'S DAMAGED GOODS AND HAS A CRAVING THAT MUST BE FED. HE'S A MILLSTONE AROUND KANE'S NECK.
HE'S ALREADY BETRAYED HIM ONCE-- AND WILL DO IT AGAIN IF IT SUITS HIM. HE'LL DRAG THEM BOTH DOWN. IT'S ONLY A MATTER OF TIME.

I'M ASSUMING IT WAS KAREL HENDRYKS WHO WAS BEHIND THE ABORTIVE KIDNAPPING? HE'S BEEN SNAPPING AT MY HEELS FOR MONTHS NOW, TO BUY INTO THE 7. HE'S THE ONLY ONE WITH THE GALL AND RESOURCES TO TRY SOMETHING LIKE THIS.
EXCEPT...IF THAT'S THE CASE, WHY HAVEN'T THEY FLED BACK UNDER HIS PROTECTION? WHY ARE THEY STILL AT LARGE? PERHAPS THEY WERE NOT CO-OPTED BUT COERCED INTO JOINING HIM?
DO THEY FEAR *HIM* MORE THAN ME? WHY DO YOU SUPPOSE THAT WOULD BE?
THERE'S ONLY ONE WAY TO FIND OUT.
INDEED. BRING ME KANE ALIVE. I WANT TO KNOW WHAT HE KNOWS ABOUT HENDRYKS.
IT...*UH*...COULD BE THAT LYNCH IS THE ONE?
DON'T BE ABSURD. THE MAN'S A WALKING CAR CRASH. I DOUBT HE CAN EVEN TIE HIS SHOES IN THE MORNING WITHOUT A FISTFUL OF PHARMACEUTICALS FIRST.
SO, IF KANE'S A KEEPER, WHAT DO YOU WANT ME TO DO WITH LYNCH?
THE SAME AS BEFORE...

"WHEN IT COMES TO MAD DOGS THERE'S ONLY ONE COURSE OF ACTION."
YOU HAPPY NOW?
I AM INDEED! RIGHT NOW, I AM THE GODDAMN POPE OF HAPPINESS!
JESUS CHRIST! I DON'T KNOW WHAT'S WORSE. YOU COMING DOWN OFF THOSE FUCKING THINGS OR YOU OUT OF YOUR FACE ON THEM!
EH, LITTLE FROM COLUMN A. LITTLE FROM COLUMN B.
AND THE ANSWER'S STILL NO. I AM *NOT* GOING TO CALL THAT CRAZY BITCH AND NEGOTIATE TURNING YOU IN FOR THE BOUNTY.
IT'D BUY US SOME TIME.
SHE HATES MY GUTS. SHE WOULDN'T BELIEVE ME AND SHE'D KILL US BOTH ANYWAY.
I'VE, *UH*... GOT AN INSTINCT FOR THESE THINGS... TRUST ME.

WE CAN'T GO BACK TO HENDRYKS. HE'S PLAYING US, I'M CERTAIN OF IT. I'VE GOT A HUNCH HE KNOWS I'VE MADE HIM...RECOGNIZED HIM AS KONRAD LEMAS.
WE GO BACK, HE'D KILL US BOTH AND JENNY. AT LEAST OUT HERE WE'VE GOT ROOM TO MANEUVER.
THIS...IS...INSANE! HOW DID THIS ALL TURN TO SHIT SO FAST?
IT HASN'T EVEN BEEN A WEEK. THE 7 WERE DEAD. I WAS HOME FREE AND SITTING ON A TON OF CASH... NOW I DON'T EVEN HAVE A POT TO PISS IN!
GO IN THE CORNER LIKE I DID. I PROMISE NOT TO LOOK. I'LL WHISTLE IF IT HELPS?
YOU THINK THIS IS A FUCKIN' JOKE, DO YOU?!
NNK!

TNKK
BEER...
WHEN DID YOU GET BEER? *WHERE* DID YOU GET BEER?
WHEN YOU WERE DITCHING THE CAR. I GOT IT FROM THAT LITTLE INDIAN PLACE ON THE CORNER.
A STORE... A STORE WITH CAMERAS...ON A STREET WITH CAMERAS! WHAT DID YOU THINK YOU WERE DOING?
SKTASHH
ARE YOU OUT OF YOUR FUCKING MIND?!
HEY!

FOR FUCK'S SAKE! WHAT'S WRONG WITH YOU?!
I STUCK MY NECK OUT SO YOU COULD GET YOUR GODDAMN HAPPY PILLS TO STOP YOU CLIMBING THE WALLS, AND YOU PULL A STUNT LIKE THIS!
WHAT'S GOING ON IN YOUR HEAD? DON'T YOU GIVE A SHIT ABOUT ANYONE OTHER THAN YOURSELF?
YOU REALLY WANT ME TO ANSWER THAT?
ENOUGH. ENOUGH OF THIS SHIT.
HEY, HEY...COME ON!
YOU MAY NOT GIVE A FLYING FUCK ABOUT ANYTHING, BUT I'VE GOT A KID OUT THERE. WHETHER SHE HATES MY GUTS OR NOT! SHE'S ALL I'VE GOT-- AND I WILL DO WHATEVER IT TAKES TO KEEP HER SAFE. UNDERSTAND?!
SCREW YOU!
WHAT...EVER... IT...TAKES. IF IT'S A CHOICE BETWEEN YOU AND HER, YOU ARE GOING TO LOSE EVERY TIME. IS THAT CLEAR?
FUCK YOU!

WHAT DID YOU SAY?
YEAH... YES...YES! IT'S FUCKIN' CLEAR!
GOOD. FINE. I'M DONE HERE. WE'RE DONE.
SO LONG, TOUGH GUY. YOU CAN WATCH YOUR OWN BACK FROM NOW ON.
PRICK.
I HEARD THAT.

CHAK-CHEK
FREEZE!
SHIT!

IT'S KANE!
DON'T BE STUPID, NOW! HE WANTS YOU ALIVE-- BUT YOU DON'T NEED TO BE IN ONE PIECE!
HENDRYKS.
TURN AROUND, HANDS BEHIND YOUR BACK.
BETTER CALL IT IN. FIGURE WE'RE DUE A BONUS FOR THIS.
DON'T HAVE TO PLAY IT SAFE NOW. OTHER ONE'S DEAD MEAT.
UNF!
YAHH!

UNNGGH
UNNGGH
UHH
KRAK
NO...
KUD
NKK...
HHT!

HKK...
HNN!
GKKL
HNFF...
HHNN
KKKK

THRRRRTT
BRAKKA
SHIT!
NOT MY PROBLEM... NOT MY GODDAMN PROBLEM...
BDAM BRRAPP BDAM
BDAM BDAMM
BDAM BDAM
HE'S OUT. LAST CLIP.
SHIT.

BRAKKA
SPAKK
SPLUT
SPAKKA
SPAKKA
C'MON, YOU FUCKIN' PUSSIES! THAT ALL YOU'VE GOT?!
THRRRRT!
BRAKKA
BRRAPP
AGH!
THUK
OW...FUCK... BASTARDS!

LIGHTS OUT, DUMBASS!
BRRRAPP
UT--
BRRR APAPAPA
IT'S KANE!
I THOUGHT YOUR BOSS WANTED ME ALIVE?!
ACCIDENTS HAPPEN, MOTHER-FUCKER!

BR
RAPP
GKKL
YOU GOOD?
EH, I'VE HAD WORSE.
MISS ME?
SHUT THE FUCK UP.
WHERE DID THEY COME FROM? I TOOK CARE OF THE ONES WHO WERE COMING UP THE STAIRS.
THEY MUST'VE COME DOWN THE OTHER WAY...FROM THE ROOF.
THE ROOF...

HELLO, BOYS.

YOU'VE GOTTA BE KIDDING...
"YOU KNOW, YOU REALLY COULDN'T MAKE THIS SHIT UP!"
SO, WHADDA WE DO NOW, BUTCH?
MAKE A BREAK FOR IT. SPLIT LEFT AND RIGHT. THEY CAN'T GET US BOTH AT THE SAME TIME.
FIFTY-FIFTY... I DON'T LIKE THOSE ODDS.
THEY'RE BETTER THAN NOTHING. READY, ON THREE.
ONE, TWO...

FSSTT ...KANE...
WHAT...?
THIS MIC'S LIVE. I KNOW YOU CAN HEAR ME. MY MEN ARE ON THEIR WAY. IF EITHER OF YOU MOVE A FUCKING MUSCLE, I'LL CUT YOU IN HALF.
IT'LL PISS HENDRYKS OFF, BUT IT'LL BE WORTH IT.
THAT'S HENDRYKS' BITCH. I THOUGHT SHE DIED.
THINK SHE'LL DO IT?
GUESS NOT.
GUESS SO.
FREEZE! STAY WHERE YOU ARE!
LOSE THE HARDWARE! DO IT!

ANY MORE BRIGHT IDEAS?
JUST ONE.
HANDS BEHIND YOUR HEAD!
CLOSE YOUR EYES.
BE GENTLE WITH ME.
SHUT THE FUCK UP AND SHOW ME THOSE HANDS, ASSHOLE!
ANYTHING YOU SAY.
PTING
THUNDERFLASH! SCOPES OFF!

FASHOOM
GIIAA!
UHUH
GO! MOVE!

TIME TO DIE, DUMBASS!
BRAKKA
BRAKKA
GKKL!
NO! NO, GODDAMMIT!
TEK
THRRRAKAKAKAK

TAKKA
SPAKKA
TEKK
MUTHERFUCKKERR!
TAKK
GO! GO!
TEKK
SPEKK
SPAKK
VIPP
ZKK
ZIKKT
WE'VE GOTTA GO DOWN!
NOT GONNA HAPPEN!

HNN! DON'T JUST STAND THERE! FUCKIN' HELP ME, WHY DON'T YOU?!
SO, IT'S TIME FOR SOME OF YOUR FUCKED-UP BRUCE WILLIS SHIT?
NO...
THIS IS SOME OF MY FUCKED-UP MACGYVER SHIT.
THIS...IS GOING TO HURT.

HHHNN!
COMING?
FUCK!
PTING
PTING
CATCH!
NO...

CHOOM
GGH
NNGGH
NNFF!
WELCOME BACK. YOU GOOD TO GO?
NO, I'M NOT FUCKING GOOD TO GO! MY HANDS ARE FUCKING HAMBURGER!
TOO BAD. BITCH ABOUT IT LATER--NOW GET OFF YOUR ASS.

NUH-AHH!
QUIET!
SCREW YOU!
UKK
ENOUGH! I'VE HAD ENOUGH OF YOUR BULLSHIT FOR ONE DAY! THIS IS YOUR LAST CHANCE. YOU GOTTA GET YOUR HEAD OUT OF YOUR ASS AND BACK IN THE GAME--
--OR I'LL PUT YOU DOWN RIGHT NOW...QUICK, CLEAN AND QUIET.
HHHNN... FUCK... YOU...
WRONG ANSWER! SEE, THIS IS ME PLAYING NICE. YOU'RE A FUCKING LIABILITY BUT THE ONLY WAY WE STAND A RAT'S ASS OF A CHANCE OF GETTING OUT OF THIS ALIVE? IS TOGETHER. BUT I CAN'T KEEP LOOKING OVER MY SHOULDER TO CHECK IF YOU'RE FUCKING UP AGAIN.
SO, CAN I COUNT ON YOU?
FOR NOW... BUT WHEN THIS IS OVER, WE GONNA HAVE THIS OUT.
FAIR ENOUGH.

SEE ANYTHING?
NOTHING. PLACE'S CLEAN. IF ANYONE'S AROUND, THEY'RE PROBABLY ALL HEADING UPSTAIRS AFTER HEARING THAT SHIT-STORM.
OKAY, WE RUN LIKE BASTARDS OUT THE FRONT, BOOST THE FIRST CAR WE FIND AND GET THE HELL OUT OF HERE.
WORKS FOR ME.
LET'S MOVE!
CRAAACK
UH!
WHAT THE FUCK--?
(ATTENTION! DROP THE WEAPONS! HANDS ABOVE YOUR HEADS!)

‹HANDS WHERE WE CAN SEE THEM. DO IT!›
IT'S THE LAW!
I GUESS THERE IS A COP AROUND WHEN YOU NEED ONE!
HEH! HA! HA HAH!
HAH! HAH! HA! HAH!
NFF...
‹QUIET!›
WHUP WHUP
‹SHIT!›
SON OF A BITCH...
WHUP WHUP

WHUP WHUP WHUP
DID YOU THINK IT WAS GOING TO BE THAT EASY?!
FFOOSHHH
PEAMMM
PEAMMM
FFOOSHHH

FOOSHH
KACHOOOM
<RETURN FIRE! BRING THAT THING DOWN!>
<GET DOWN, YOU ASSHOLE!>
KKKL!
THRRRRTTTT

WE'VE GOTTA BOOK! WE'RE SITTING DUCKS HERE!
GO! BACK UP-- BACK INSIDE!
BLAM BLAM
BRAAP BDAMM
FUCK!
AAH!

WELL, THIS FEELS DEPRESSINGLY FAMILIAR.
PUCKER UP, PANSIES!
CHOOM
KTAANG

CAUGH... CAUGH BASTARDS...
IT'S NO GOOD...IT'S ARMORED!
WE'LL SEE. HIT IT AGAIN!
STAND CLEAR! FIRING!
FTOOSSHHHH
FASHOOM

I'VE SEEN ENOUGH OF THIS FLOORSHOW. TIME TO BE GONE.
I HEAR THAT!
THERE! I SEE THEM!
BRING ME KANE. DO WHAT YOU WANT WITH THE OTHER ONE.
SIR!
OH, FOR GOD'S SAKE!
DO I HAVE TO DO EVERYTHING MYSELF?!

TEK
BLAMM
GAH!
SPUKK
SURPRISE!
NO...

SKDAMM
BRAKK KRAKK
NNH!
MM
FASHOO

HHHH...
HEY, HOW ABOUT THAT? THE PUNCHY LITTLE PISSANT'S STILL BREATHING.
SOON PUT THAT RIGHT.
NO, NOT YET...WE NEED HIM ALIVE.

EH, IT'LL KEEP.
CLUDD
GRAB A LEG...
DO I GET TO MAKE A WISH?
BETTER...
...WE'RE GOING TO PAY THE DOCTOR A HOUSE CALL.

IT'S NOT GONNA WORK.
IT'LL WORK.
NO WAY.
IT'LL WORK!
WE'VE GOT A CHANCE TO SHAKE THIS SHIT FROM OFF OUR HEELS AND GET THE HELL OUT OF DODGE, AND YOU WANT TO GO STICK YOUR HEAD IN THE LION'S MOUTH?! IT'S BULLSHIT!
IT'LL BE A WALK IN THE PARK.
BESIDES...

...I'VE GOT A PLAN.

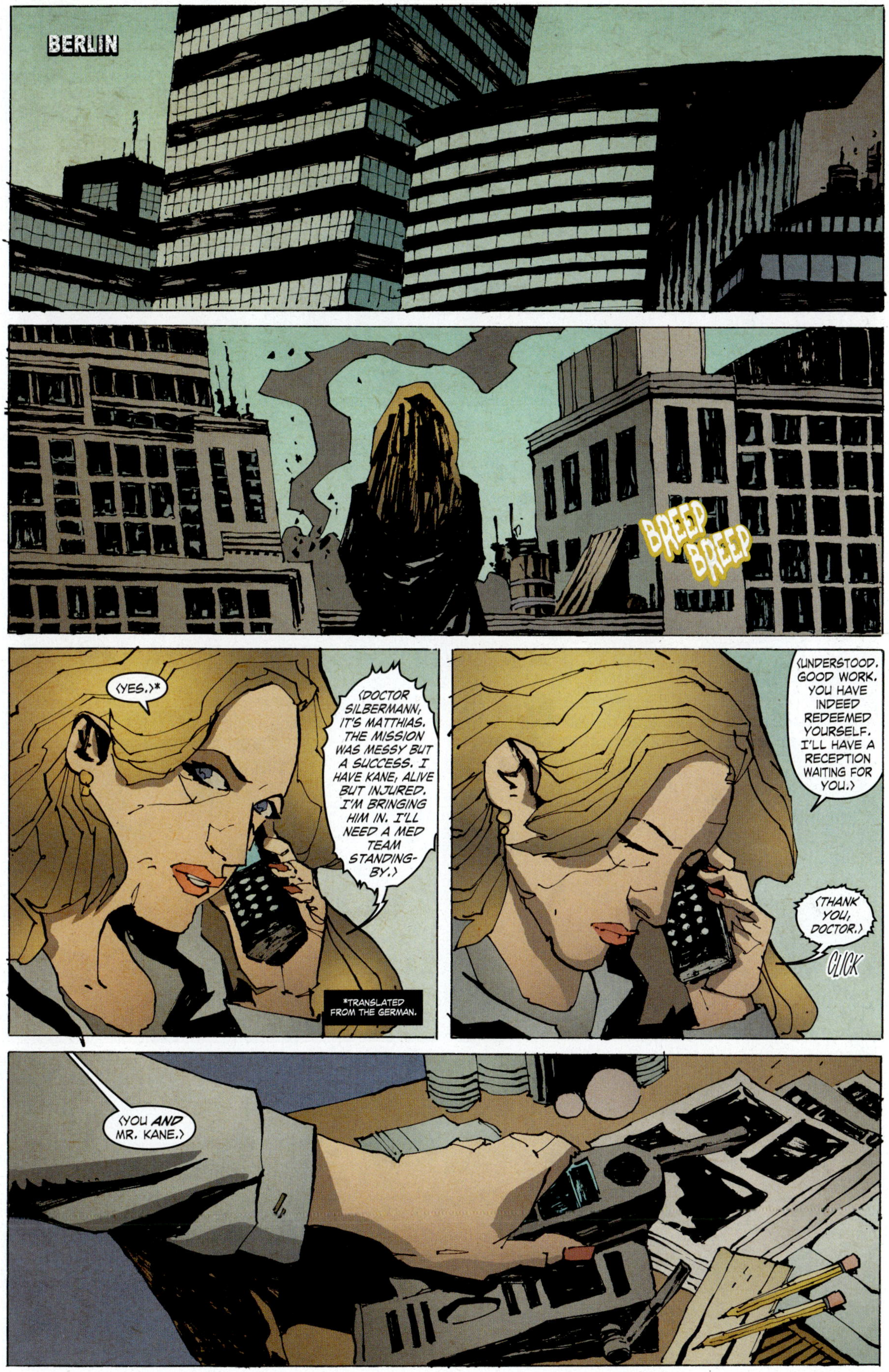
BERLIN
BREEP BREEP
‹YES.›*
‹DOCTOR SILBERMANN, IT'S MATTHIAS. THE MISSION WAS MESSY BUT A SUCCESS. I HAVE KANE; ALIVE BUT INJURED. I'M BRINGING HIM IN. I'LL NEED A MED TEAM STANDING-BY.›
*TRANSLATED FROM THE GERMAN.
‹UNDERSTOOD. GOOD WORK. YOU HAVE INDEED REDEEMED YOURSELF. I'LL HAVE A RECEPTION WAITING FOR YOU.›
‹THANK YOU, DOCTOR.›
CLICK
‹YOU AND MR. KANE.›

MUCH OBLIGED, CUPCAKE.
THAT WAS POINTLESS. SHE WON'T HAVE BELIEVED ME. SHE'LL BE EXPECTING YOU!
I KNOW...
"...IN FACT, I'M COUNTING ON IT."
‹GO! GO! GO!›

<HANDS WHERE I CAN SEE THEM!>
MMPHH! GMMPHH!
<WHAT THE HELL?!>
<JESUS CHRIST! GET HIM OUT OF THERE!>
GMMHH!
SHRIPP
PTINK

FAA
SHOOMMM
THOOM
CHOOM

<OH GOD...OH, MY GOD!>
<TERRORISTS! IT'S TERRORISTS!>
AND THE CROWD GOES WILD. I DIDN'T FIGURE HE'D ROLL OVER SO EASY.
HE DIDN'T. HE KNEW HE WAS A DEAD MAN EITHER WAY. THE GOOD DOCTOR DOESN'T DO FAILURE. 'LEAST THIS WAY HE FIGURED HE'D DO THE NOBLE THING AND FALL ON HIS SWORD. LET HER KNOW WE WERE COMING.
NOBLE MY ASS.
<HEY! YOU TWO, STEP BACK HERE, NOW!>

‹SHOW ME SOME I.D.! WHERE DO YOU THINK YOU'RE GOING?›
GOIN' UP!
KA-CHOOM
KANE!

‹SECURITY, THIS IS SILBERMANN! WHAT THE HELL IS GOING ON DOWN THERE? WE KNEW HE WAS COMING SO WHY ARE YOU FUCKING AROUND?!›
‹I WANT THE BUILDING SEALED! LOCK OFF THE ELEVATORS. SHUT US DOWN TIGHT, SEAL HIM IN AND RUN A SWEEP, FLOOR BY FLOOR.›
‹BUT DOCTOR, THE POLICE, THE EMERGENCY SERVICES-- THEY'LL REQUIRE ACCESS...›
‹JUST DO IT!›
SEE, IT'S WORKING.
EH, I STILL SAY THIS SUCKS ASS. WE'RE IN THE DOOR BUT THERE'S NO WAY WE'RE GONNA GET TO THAT KRAUT BITCH.
TOLD YOU.
RELAX, IT'S NOTHING.
I'VE GOT IT COVERED.

"WE'RE TAKING THE SCENIC ROUTE."
PANGG
‹WHAT DO YOU MEAN THERE'S NO SIGN OF THEM?!›
‹DOCTOR, WE...›
‹THEY DIDN'T BLOW THE BUILDING HALF-TO-HELL FOR THE FUN OF IT! THEY'RE PROFESSIONALS...KANE IS AT LEAST. IT WAS A DIVERSION, THEY'RE HERE SOMEWHERE...›
‹FIND... THEM.›
GUTEN TAG!
TEK

BEEP
UHH!
KA-SHOOM
JESUS!

DOCTOR SILBERMANN, I PRESUME! IF YOU'RE ARMED, I SUGGEST YOU TOSS IT OVER.
BLAM BLAM BLAM
SPAKK
TEKK
CHAKK
MIND IF I GIVE IT A GO?
BE MY GUEST.
BRAKKA BRAKKA BRAKKA
HE SAID LOSE THE PIECE, BITCH!
TEKK CHEKK
CHAKK
CHUKK
ALL RIGHT! ALL RIGHT!
I'M COMING OUT!

I HAVE TO ADMIT, KANE. I UNDERESTIMATED YOU. I'M IMPRESSED THAT YOU GOT THIS FAR. OF COURSE YOU REALIZE MY MEN ARE ALREADY ON THEIR WAY. THEY'LL BE HERE ANY MINUTE.
WE WON'T TAKE THAT LONG.
SO, YOU MEAN TO KILL ME?
THAT REMAINS TO BE SEEN.
ON WHAT EXACTLY? WHAT IS IT YOU WANT?
TO BE LEFT ALONE, ME AND MY DAUGHTER.
AND ME.
AND HIM.
I DON'T GIVE A SHIT ABOUT THE 7 AND ALL OF THIS...THIS BULLSHIT! JUST LIFT THE BOUNTY AND LET US BE ON OUR WAY.
THAT'S IT?
YES. YOUR LIFE FOR OURS.

AND WHAT GUARANTEE DO I HAVE YOU SIMPLY WON'T KILL ME AFTERWARDS?
YOU DON'T. YOU'VE ONLY GOT MY WORD. SAME AS I'LL HAVE YOURS YOU WON'T COME AFTER US WHEN WE'RE GONE.
VERY WELL THEN. LET ME SEE WHAT I CAN DO... PROVIDING THIS THING STILL WORKS.
AH, HERE WE GO...
...THERE. DONE. SIMPLE.
THAT'S IT?
THAT'S IT. THE PRESS OF A COUPLE OF KEYS AND YOUR LIFE'S YOUR OWN AGAIN.
NOW WE WASTE HER?
WHAT?! C'MON, AFTER WHAT SHE DID TO US?!
NO, GODDAMMIT!

THAT WILL ALWAYS BE YOUR WEAKNESS, KANE, YOUR ACHILLES HEEL. YOUR ANTIQUATED, MISPLACED SENSE OF MORALITY. YOU BELIEVE THAT THERE'S STILL HONOR AMONG THIEVES.
SOMETHING LIKE THAT.
IT'S A PITY MR. LYNCH DOESN'T SUBSCRIBE TO THE SAME THEORY. FOR EXAMPLE, IF HE'D HAD HIS WAY...
SCREW THIS!
THRRRKT
WHAT DID YOU DO! I GAVE HER MY WORD!
I DIDN'T! WHAT'VE YOU GOT T'BITCH ABOUT?! YOU'RE HEAD OF THE 7 NOW. YOU'RE KING OF THE FUCKING HILL!
WHUDDTCH
GYAHH!

NFF!
PTUHH!
WELL NOW, I GUESS IT'S THAT TIME!
GUESS SO.
YAHH!
GNKK!
HGKK!

KRAKK
DAMN, THIS IS GOING TO BE EASIER THAN I THOUGHT. SHE WAS RIGHT, YOU ARE A PUSSY!
HHH...
CHUD
GIAAH!
AND YOU HAVEN'T GOT THE BRAINS TO KNOW WHEN YOU'RE BEING PLAYED!
WHUDD THUDD CHUDD
UKK...
WH UKK
GNNN...

NFFH...
WHAT D'YOU KNOW?! LEAST SHE WAS GOOD FOR SOMETHING.
SON OF A...
DON'T!
DON'T MAKE ME KILL YOU! I SWEAR TO GOD, DON'T BE AN ASSHOLE!
POINT TAKEN. SO WHAT HAPPENS NOW?
WE CALL IT EVEN AND YOU LEAVE.

YOU'RE KIDDING! THERE'S A FUCKING ARMY BETWEEN HERE AND THE GROUND FLOOR!
NOT MY PROBLEM. GO...NOW.
THE LAST FUCKING BOY SCOUT, EH? SO WHAT ARE YOU GONNA DO?
ME? YOU WON'T BE SURPRISED, I'M GOING TO FIND MY GIRL.
LONDON
"BUT FIRST, I'M GOING TO TAKE CARE OF BUSINESS."

MR. HENDRYKS, BREAKFAST, SIR.
LEAVE IT THERE.
I'M SORRY TO DISTURB YOU FURTHER, SIR, BUT THERE'S SOMETHING THAT REQUIRES YOUR URGENT ATTENTION.
YES? WHAT IS IT?
MY RESIGNATION!
BLAM BLAM BLAM
IT'S ME. IT'S DONE.
WHERE DO I PICK UP MY MONEY?
TEN MILLION
THE END

KANE & LYNCH 1 *cover*

KANE & LYNCH 5 *cover*

ME

THOOM

FROM INDIE COMICS SENSATION

BRIAN WOOD

"Measures up to any summer blockbuster."
–TIME OUT NEW YORK

"The dramatic images recall the nightly news, and stories of warzone life ring true. **GRADE: A-"**
– ENTERTAINMENT WEEKLY

"One of the strongest ongoing series to come out of DC's Vertigo line in some time. **GRADE: A-"**
–THE ONION

VOL. 1: ON THE GROUND
VOL. 2: BODY OF A JOURNALIST
VOL. 3: PUBLIC WORKS
VOL. 4: FRIENDLY FIRE
VOL. 5: THE HIDDEN WAR
VOL. 6: BLOOD IN THE GAME
VOL. 7: WAR POWERS
VOL. 8: HEARTS AND MINDS

DMZ VOL. 2:
BODY OF A JOURNALIST

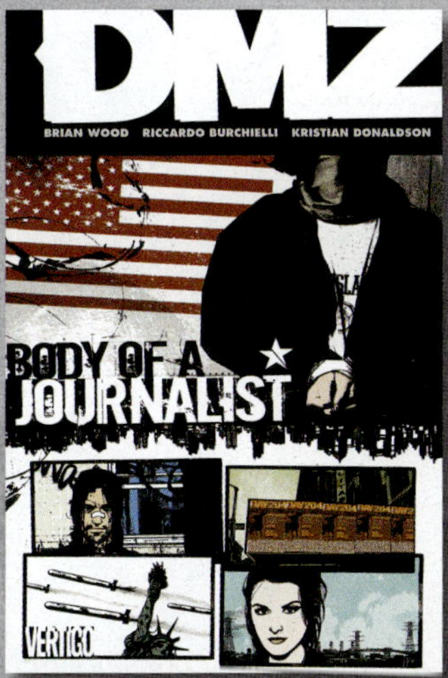

DMZ VOL. 3:
PUBLIC WORKS

DMZ VOL. 4:
FRIENDLY FIRE

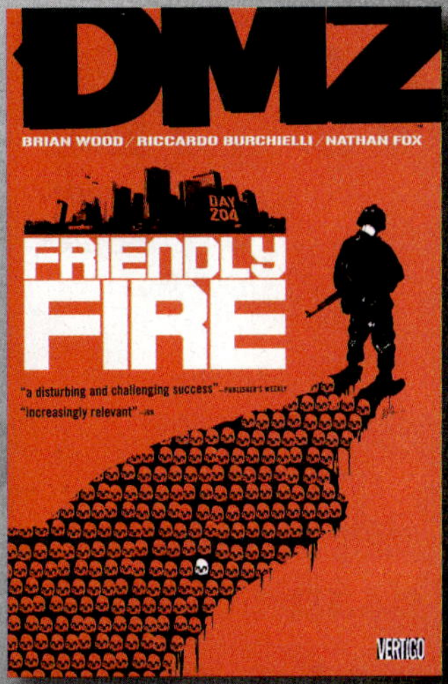

GO TO
VERTIGOBOOKS.COM
FOR FREE SAMPLES OF THE FIRST ISSUES OF OUR GRAPHIC NOVELS

Suggested for Mature Readers

"The best new series in years."
– GARTH ENNIS

JASON AARON

with R.M. GUERA

"One of the richest, most rewarding reads around."
– WIZARD

"SCALPED still rises to the top of the Vertigo pack every month. . . . Intense."
– IGN.com

"One of the best comics ever created."
– PHILADELPHIA DAILY NEWS

VOL. 1: INDIAN COUNTRY
VOL. 2: CASINO BOOGIE
VOL. 3: DEAD MOTHERS
VOL. 4: THE GRAVEL IN YOUR GUTS
VOL. 5: HIGH LONESOME
VOL. 6: THE GNAWING

SCALPED VOL. 2:
CASINO BOOGIE

SCALPED VOL. 3:
DEAD MOTHERS

SCALPED VOL. 4:
THE GRAVEL IN YOUR GUTS

GO TO
VERTIGOBOOKS.COM
FOR FREE SAMPLES OF THE FIRST ISSUES OF OUR GRAPHIC NOVELS

Suggested for Mature Readers